For Craig.
The most magical part of Christmas
is spending it with you.

THIS BOOK BELONGS TO:

....

WITH LOVE FROM:

....

Children's books by Megan Hess

Claris: The Chicest Mouse in Paris
Claris: Fashion Show Fiasco
Claris: Bonjour Riviera
Claris: Holiday Heist
Claris: Palace Party

Oli and Basil: The Dashing Frogs of Travel

Where is Claris in Paris!
Where is Claris in New York!

HardieGrant
CHILDREN'S PUBLISHING

Claris: Holiday Heist
first published in 2020 by
Hardie Grant Children's Publishing
Wurundjeri Country
Ground Floor, Building 1, 658 Church Street
Richmond, Victoria 3121, Australia
www.hardiegrantchildrenspublishing.com

Designed by Pooja Desai

A catalogue record for this
book is available from the
National Library of Australia

ISBN: 9781760504953

Hardie Grant acknowledges the Traditional Owners of the country on which we
work, the Wurundjeri people of the Kulin nation and the Gadigal people of the
Eora nation, and recognises their continuing connection to the land, waters and
culture. We pay our respects to their Elders past, present and emerging.

Printed in China through Leo Paper Group

3 5 7 9 10 8 6 4

Claris

THE CHICEST MOUSE IN PARIS

Holiday Heist

Megan Hess

In New York for winter was chic little Claris.
She'd travelled so far from her *maison* in Paris!

With her friend by her side – a cat called Monsieur –
Christmas would be a dream, of that she was sure.

The whole family loved prepping their New York abode
for the holiday season, while outside it snowed.

Well, all except one – their daughter, the Brat,
who could make a big fuss at the drop of a hat.

'Where are MY other gifts?' she screeched in dismay.
'We have to go out to buy lots more, TODAY!'

While Madame calmed down her terrible Brat,
Monsieur pricked an ear. 'Oh, did you hear that?
What fabulous news! We're out for the day.
To Fifth Avenue and then Bergdorf's cafe.'

Claris clapped with delight. 'Manhattan won't wait!
Now, to choose a fun look for this *très* lovely date.'

A fashion show was afoot as she tried to decide
on the most festive look for the Upper East Side.

A Valentino cape would be perfect for snow,
with some fluffy Chanel, or a Fendi with bows!

Soon Madame was calling her driver outside,
and Claris saw something she couldn't abide.

Some small mice were shivering, no shoes on their feet;
they were hiding away from the wind and the sleet.
They asked, chattering, 'Can you spare some food, please?'

'Oh dear,' Claris said. 'I am all out of cheese!'

Before she could find the right way to assist,
the car had arrived and off she was whisked.

Claris held Monsieur's paw; she was feeling quite blue.
She'd wanted to help them, but what could she do?

They soon came to a store, wrapped in bows with great flair.
It was magical, beautiful – New York's Cartier!

As the Brat made a beeline for jewels shining bright,
Claris was drawn to an interesting sight.

A man at the counter, so vintage and chic:
'Can you polish this ring? It's a precious antique.

'It's my wife's wedding band – fifty years we're united!
It's a family heirloom. She will be so delighted.'

Claris watched in awe and held back her tears.
How splendid, she thought, *to be loved all those years.*

He left the ring on the glass, but what caught her eye?
Why, a paw from a bag. It was ever so sly!

The paw snatched the ring at incredible speed.
Our mouse gave a gasp. What a horrible deed!

Yet the bag's stylish owner did not seem to know
that she harboured a thief – quite clearly a pro.

Claris and Monsieur, without missing a beat,
went after the woman out onto the street.

The woman walked fast, her Louboutins click-clacking.
The chase was now on and it was nerve-racking!

She hailed a cab. Upper East? Lower West?
Either way, our two heroes would not stop their quest!

'Quick, Claris, jump! They can't get away.
This taxi's about to take off for Broadway!'

As they zoomed through New York, past the lights of Times Square,
no-one noticed this unlikely crime-busting pair.

The taxi pulled up at a grand old townhouse.
'Come on, Monsieur!' said our brave little mouse.

'Follow my lead, I've a plan that's foolproof –
a window is open, up there on the roof.'

They scurried and darted from the rail to the ledge.
Stopping this burglar was Claris's pledge.

LOOT MANOR

They burst through the window and were shocked to see
the spoils of this thief's elaborate crime spree!

The smug cat lay sprawled in a jewel-covered nest.
Liz Taylor herself would have been so impressed!

He admired the ring that he'd stolen that morn,
then cast it aside with the others and yawned.

Claris quickly marched over and seized back the ring.
'You are busted, cat burglar, and I must say one thing:
You're not just stealing jewellery,
but breaking the hearts
of people in love –
tearing memories apart.'

The thief startled, then let out a frightening growl.
'Get out, little mouse, or I'll eat you!' he yowled.

Monsieur bared his teeth and the burglar shrank back.
It seemed Claris was safe from becoming his snack!

With the ring in her clutches, Claris was sure
they were ready to finish this little detour!

As they left, she hoped they had planted the seed
that the thief should retire from his incessant greed.

'Let's take back this ring! It's high time we split.
Cartier closes soon, so let's step on it!'

They hitched a ride back with a nice horse named Dazzle,
arranged by their French friends, Oli and Basil.

As they passed Central Park, Claris polished the ring
so the man could collect it that same evening.

At Cartier, the brat could be heard from outside,
still wanting more gifts though the bows were all tied.

'I want more!' the Brat screamed. 'It's all about me!
I don't have enough. Oh, why can't you SEE?'

Her nasty explosion gave Claris a chance
to return the man's ring without drawing a glance.

As they stood on the sidewalk awaiting their car,
Claris saw a white flash darting in from afar.

It was there for one second but then lost to sight,
and moving so fast, it gave Claris a fright!

The doorman looked down: all these jewels had appeared!
But WHO did they come from? How terribly weird.

Claris realised the cat might be changing his ways,
and giving up theft till the end of his days!

From Fifth to Tribeca, past New York's best art,
our pair taught a thief to remember his heart.

It was time to go home, as a good deed was done.
What an adventure! And oh, so much fun.

'Merry Christmas,' said Monsieur. 'Your heart is so true.
You are so kind to others, now here's something for you.'

Claris opened the box and found her favourite cheese.
She smiled and gave him a big mousey squeeze.

Her face filled with joy and she suddenly knew.
'There is one last thing that we just have to do …'

Claris and Monsieur found those mice in the cold
and brought them some cheese, warmth and baubles in gold.

Claris didn't have much, but still plenty to share.
It's important in life to show that you care.

What matters the most is not what you can take
but good times with friends. Oh, the memories you'll make!

The new friends all laughed as snow fell from above.
And Claris knew that the meaning of Christmas was love.

Megan Hess is an acclaimed art director
and illustrator who works with some of the
most prestigious designers and luxury brands
around the world, such as Chanel, Dior, Cartier
and Tiffany & Co. Megan has also written seven
best-selling books for adults. To see all her
books, visit MeganHess.com.

Holiday Heist is the fourth book
in her beloved *Claris* collection.

Explore the *World of Claris* at ClarisTheMouse.com and
follow the adventures on Instagram @claristhemouse